**Put Beginning Readers on the Right Track with
ALL ABOARD READING™**

The All Aboard Reading series is especially designed for beginning readers. Written by noted authors and illustrated in full color, these are books that children really want to read—books to excite their imagination, expand their interests, make them laugh, and support their feelings. With fiction and nonfiction stories that are high interest and curriculum-related, All Aboard Reading books offer something for every young reader. And with four different reading levels, the All Aboard Reading series lets you choose which books are most appropriate for your children and their growing abilities.

Picture Readers
Picture Readers have super-simple texts, with many nouns appearing as rebus pictures. At the end of each book are 24 flash cards—on one side is a rebus picture; on the other side is the written-out word.

Station Stop 1
Station Stop 1 books are best for children who have just begun to read. Simple words and big type make these early reading experiences more comfortable. Picture clues help children to figure out the words on the page. Lots of repetition throughout the text helps children to predict the next word or phrase—an essential step in developing word recognition.

Station Stop 2
Station Stop 2 books are written specifically for children who are reading with help. Short sentences make it easier for early readers to understand what they are reading. Simple plots and simple dialogue help children with reading comprehension.

Station Stop 3
Station Stop 3 books are perfect for children who are reading alone. With longer text and harder words, these books appeal to children who have mastered basic reading skills. More complex stories captivate children who are ready for more challenging books.

In addition to All Aboard Reading books, look for All Aboard Math Readers™ (fiction stories that teach math concepts children are learning in school); All Aboard Science Readers™ (nonfiction books that explore the most fascinating science topics in age-appropriate language); and All Aboard Poetry Readers™ (funny, rhyming poems for readers of all levels).

All Aboard for happy reading!

Visit <u>www.strawberryshortcake.com</u>
to join the Friendship Club and
redeem your Strawberry Shortcake
Berry Points for "berry" fun stuff!

Strawberry Shortcake™ © 2004 by Those Characters From Cleveland, Inc. Used under license by Penguin Young Readers Group. All rights reserved. Published by Grosset & Dunlap, a division of Penguin Young Readers Group, 345 Hudson Street, New York, New York 10014. GROSSET & DUNLAP and ALL ABOARD READING are trademarks of Penguin Group (USA) Inc. Printed in the U.S.A.

Library of Congress Cataloging-in-Publication Data

Bryant, Megan E.
  Berry thankful! / by Megan E. Bryant ; illustrated by SI Artists.
    p. cm. — (All aboard reading. Station stop 1)
  "Strawberry Shortcake."
  Summary: When Strawberry Shortcake invites her friends for dinner, they all stop to be grateful for food and friendship and more.
  ISBN 0-448-43517-9 (pbk.)
  [1. Gratitude—Fiction.] I. S.I. Artists (Group) II. Title. III. Series.
  PZ7.B79Ber 2004
  [E]—dc22
                        2003024919

ISBN 0-448-43517-9   10 9 8 7 6 5 4 3 2 1

Berry Thankful!

By Megan E. Bryant
Illustrated by SI Artists

Grosset & Dunlap • New York

Strawberry Shortcake
is berry excited.

Her friends are coming over
for dinner.

Strawberry Shortcake gets
the house ready.

Strawberry Shortcake gets
the food ready.

Strawberry Shortcake
gets herself ready!

Ding-dong!

Who is at the door?

It's Strawberry Shortcake's friends!

Ginger Snap made stuffing.

Huckleberry Pie made
mashed potatoes.

Orange Blossom made
peas and carrots.

Angel Cake made pie.

Ginger Snap looks around.
There is so much
to be thankful for.

Then she has an idea.

What is everyone thankful for?

Ginger Snap gives thanks
for friends.

Strawberry Shortcake
is thankful for friends, too.

Huckleberry Pie gives thanks
for good food.

Strawberry Shortcake
is thankful for good food, too.

Orange Blossom gives thanks
for plants.

Strawberry Shortcake
is thankful
for plants, too.

Angel Cake gives thanks
for her pet.

Strawberry Shortcake is thankful
for her pets, too.

Strawberry Shortcake
is thankful for so much.

How will she pick one thing?

Strawberry Shortcake
has an idea.

She knows what she is thankful for . . . everything!

What are <u>you</u> thankful for?

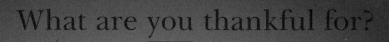